HAUNTED
NATCHEZ

HAUNTED NATCHEZ

ALAN BROWN

Haunted America

Published by Haunted America
A Division of The History Press
Charleston, SC 29403
www.historypress.net

Copyright © 2010 by Alan Brown
All rights reserved

First published 2010

All images are courtesy of the author.

Manufactured in the United States

ISBN 978.1.59629.928.3

Library of Congress Cataloging-in-Publication Data

Brown, Alan, 1950 Jan. 12-
Haunted Natchez / Alan Brown.
p. cm.
Includes bibliographical references (p.).
ISBN 978-1-59629-928-3
1. Haunted places--Mississippi--Natchez. 2. Ghosts--Mississippi--
Natchez. I. Title.
BF1472.U6B 7429 2010
133.109762'26--dc22
2010028289

CONTENTS

CONTENTS

ACKNOWLEDGEMENTS

I would like to thank Mary Emrick and Jeanette Feltus for the information they gave me for this project. I am also indebted to my informants who preferred to remain anonymous. I am grateful to Greg Jones, Kenny Reynolds and Cole Walker for sharing their computer knowledge with me. I would like to recommend Natchez Ghost Tours, which provides visitors with a good overview of the city's ghost stories in the comfort of a tour bus. Finally, I am indebted to my wife, Marilyn, whose presence makes my trips to haunted places even more enjoyable.

ARLINGTON

One of the most prominent of Natchez's pioneering families was the Surget family. Pierre Surget was born in 1731 in Rochelle, France. As a young man, Pierre worked as a ship's captain. In the 1780s, he received a Spanish land grant of twenty-five hundred acres southeast of Natchez, Mississippi. At the same time, he moved his wife, Catherine, and their eleven children from Louisiana to Mississippi, which became their permanent home. Three of his children—Captain Francis Surget, James Surget and Jane Surget White—became prominent landowners and citizens of Natchez. Pierre went on to acquire large landholdings in Arkansas, Louisiana and Mississippi. He and his other family members owned hundreds of slaves, who worked in the cotton and cornfields.

The Surget family sold their cotton through agents in Liverpool, England, and New Orleans. They also held

Arlington.

bank accounts in New York and New Orleans and loaned money to landowners in the Natchez area.

In the years prior to the Civil War, members of the Surget family eventually intermarried with other landowning families in the area. Many people living in Natchez today remember Pierre Surget primarily because of his connection to one of the city's most significant—and legendary—antebellum homes.

In 1816, construction began on a home for Pierre Surget's eldest daughter, Mrs. Jane White. In 1820, Mrs. White moved into her beautiful Federal-style villa. Tragically, she died after spending only one night in her beautiful home. Her sister, Mrs. Bingaman, inherited the house, the property and all of the furnishings. Five generations of the Surget family lived at Arlington and added to its store of luxurious furnishings. By 1977, Arlington still contained a three-hundred-year-old spinet piano, objets d'art and a library consisting of thousands of books.

Even though Arlington was designated a National Historic Landmark in 1974, it was an abandoned wreck by the late 1990s. In 2001, a devastating fire destroyed the rear gallery, which had been added after the home was first constructed. The roof was destroyed as well, but the rooms in the main house were undamaged. The owner of the old mansion, the Historic Natchez Foundation (HNF), installed a new roof and rafters and took additional measures to stabilize the house. Still, Arlington is a sad shadow of its former self. All of the windows are broken, and much of the exterior and interior has been marred by spray-painted graffiti. At the time of this writing, the HNF was in the process of installing an alarm system to protect the house from further vandalism.

The ghost story that members of the Surget family passed down from one generation to the next has become as faded as the house itself. For years, people said that every night at the stroke of midnight, a ghostly carriage drove up the long drive and pulled up at the main entrance of Arlington. The door opened, and a beautiful woman climbed out, walked up the steps and passed through the unopened front door.

Most people believe that the specter was the ghost of Jane White, who never had the opportunity to spend much time in her beautiful home while she was alive. One can only hope that after Arlington has been fully restored, its signature ghost story will be revived as well.

DUNLEITH

In 1777, a Welsh immigrant named Jeremiah Routh moved his wife and four children to Spanish West Florida in the Natchez District, where he had received a land grant of five hundred acres. In 1791, Routh traveled to Ohio to buy lumber for a two-story frame house. The flatboat on which the lumber had been loaded arrived at Natchez-Under-the-Hill just as a storm was brewing. The next morning, the flatboat and its cargo were gone.

Routh reported the theft to the governor of the post of Natchez. A scoundrel named Olivarez said that the flatboat had come loose from its moorings during the storm, and he claimed the craft and its cargo by right of salvage. Apparently, the stress proved to be too much for Jeremiah Routh. He died in 1791, and the estate was left to his two sons, Job and Jeremiah R., who divided up the property.

Several years later, a judge ordered Olivarez to reimburse Job Routh for the cost of the stolen lumber. Following his marriage to Anne Madeline Miller on May 30, 1792, Job purchased additional acreage with the intention of growing cotton on it. He also acquired a seventeen-hundred-acre land grant south of the center of Natchez. Over the years, Job sold off most of his landholdings, except for the fifty acres on which he had built Routhland. John Routh died of debility on December 12, 1834. His property, including his slaves, was divided among his nine children.

Routh's daughter Mary, who had married a wealthy planter named Thomas Ellis in 1829, when she was sixteen, inherited Routhland. After Thomas Ellis died in 1839, Mary married a Natchez banker named Charles Dahlgren. Dahlgren immediately took control of Job Routh's holdings in Mississippi and Louisiana and settled all of his father-in-law's debts. On August 18, 1855, the Dahlgrens' fortunes, which had been steadily rising since their marriage, were drastically reversed when their home, Routhland, burned down while they were vacationing in Beersheba Springs, Tennessee.

Dahlgren decided to start all over by building an entirely new mansion where Routhland once stood. He used a plan for a Greek Revival mansion that appeared in the book *The Architecture of Country Houses* (1856) by Alexander Jackson Davis and Andrew Jackson Downing. The mansion was constructed between 1856 and 1857. The exterior was lined with twenty-six Doric columns. The five-story mansion included a cellar, two parlors, four bedrooms, a

Dunleith.

library, a dining room and an attic with dormer windows. The kitchen, laundry and slaves' quarters were located in a building in the back. In a cruel twist of fate, Mary Dahlgren spent only three months in her new home before dying of heart trouble in March 1858. She was forty-five years old. Charles Dahlgren put the new Routhland up for sale in March 1858.

On January 4, 1858, Alfred Vidal Davis purchased Routhland from Charles Dahlgren. He immediately renamed his new home Dunleith. After the Civil War broke out in 1861, Davis formed a volunteer infantry company called the Natchez Rifles. His troop later became part of the Fourteenth Louisiana Infantry. Davis's wife, Sarah, joined up with her husband's regiment on the way to Richmond. She left one of her household slaves, Catherine White, in charge of Dunleith in her absence. When Davis returned to Dunleith in 1863, Natchez was under the control of the Yankees. His wife Sarah died two years later.

Dunleith had a number of different owners after the Civil War. Alfred Vidal Davis sold the mansion to Hiram M. Baldwin in 1866. Following Baldwin's sudden death in 1868, Dunleith was sold to John R. Stockton. In 1886, Dunleith was sold once again, this time to Joseph Neibert Carpenter for $20,000. Carpenter made a fortune by investing in a hardware store, a grocery store, railroad and steamboat lines and cottonseed oil mills. He and his family made generous donations to Natchez schools over the years. The Carpenter family owned Dunleith until 1976.

Dunleith has been on the National Register of Historic Places since 1935. In 1976, Dunleith was purchased by William Heins and converted into a bed-and-breakfast. In 1999, Mrs. Edward Worley and her son, Michael Worley, spent a considerable amount of time and money renovating the old mansion. The antebellum mansion's signature ghost story focuses on a harp that once stood in the front parlor.

Dunleith is haunted by a relative of Mrs. Charles Dahlgren, remembered today only as "Miss Percy." In her book, *13 Mississippi Ghosts and Jeffrey*, writer Kathryn Tucker says that Miss Percy fell in love with a dashing young

Frenchman. Some people say that he was a count; others believe that he was a high-ranking French officer. The two were inseparable, and many people believed that a wedding was in the planning stages. One day, the Frenchman professed his undying love for Miss Percy, but the smile on her face immediately turned into a frown when he said that he was going to have to return to France on business. Promising that he would return to her soon, he kissed her and disappeared into the night.

Months passed without a word from her lover. Finally, Miss Percy decided to travel to France to find out why she had not received any letters from her paramour. Several weeks later, Miss Percy returned from Europe, her head bowed in shame. Her lover had fallen in love with someone else in France but did not have the heart to tell Miss Percy. She returned to Dunleith and lived in an upstairs bedroom. Every afternoon, she walked downstairs to the front parlor and strummed melancholy songs on the harp. For years, she repeated this sad ritual before finally dying in Dunleith.

For over a century, people staying at Dunleith claim to have heard the faint tones of harp music coming from the front parlor. When I stayed at Dunleith in August 2009, a tour guide told me that one morning in 2008, a guest complained that she had been awakened in the middle of the night by someone playing a harp in the parlor. The harp is not the one owned by the Dahlgren family. The Worley family purchased it in about 2000. The tour guide showed the harp to the guest, who realized that it was in

The first-floor parlor and harp at Dunleith.

such poor condition that no one would have been able to play it. The tour guide then related the tragic tale of Miss Percy, the lonely woman who continues to drown her sorrows in music.

GLENBURNIE

Before the development of the surrounding subdivision, Glenburnie was located in the middle of a sprawling plantation. Nearby was another impressive antebellum home called Glenwood. The incredible story of these two houses rivals any of the southern gothic works of Flannery O'Connor, Carson McCullers or Tennessee Williams. On August 4, 1932, the lives of the two families who lived in these houses converged in a memorable but ultimately tragic way.

Jane Surget Merrill—or Jennie, as she preferred to be called—was born in 1864 to Ayres Merrill and Jane Surget Merrill. Jennie was the granddaughter of one of the first settlers in the Natchez area, Pierre Surget. She was also the granddaughter of William Dunbar, a Natchez planter, scientist and inventor. Jennie's father had shown hospitality to Ulysses S. Grant and his soldiers during the Civil War.

Glenburnie.

Grant returned the favor after he became president by appointing Ayers Merrill ambassador to Belgium. Jennie, who was educated in Brussels by private tutors, was the darling of high society in Europe. She was even presented to Queen Victoria at the Court of St. James. After her father became ill, he and his family returned to their home, Elms Court, in Natchez.

Following the death of her father in 1883, Jennie moved from Elms Court to a series of antebellum mansions, including Glenwood, before finally settling in at Glenburnie in 1904. Built in 1834, Glenburnie was a multiroom mansion located on forty-five acres of land.

Some people say that Jennie moved to Glenburnie to be close to her second cousin, Duncan Minor. They were said to have been in love, but they could never marry because the Surgets and the Minors had been feuding since the Civil War. Duncan's mother threatened to disinherit him if he married Jennie, so he rode out to Glenburnie each night on horseback but returned home the next morning before breakfast. Over time, Jennie became a recluse, seeing no one except Duncan.

Jennie's closest neighbor was Richard Dana, son of an Episcopalian minister. He was an accomplished pianist with a promising career as a concert pianist in his future. Tragically, his hopes of achieving fame were dashed forever when a window sash fell on his hand, permanently disabling his fingers. As a young man, "Dick" Dana became close friends with Jennie and Duncan. In the 1890s, Dick fell in love with a ravishing redhead named Octavia Dockery, who was an accomplished poet and author. Her works were published in the *New York World* newspaper and in various magazines. She was also the first woman in Natchez to ride astride a horse like a man. After the death of her parents, she moved in with Dick Dana at Glenwood.

As time passed, Octavia and Dick became increasingly eccentric. Octavia cooked their meals over the fireplace and made clothes for them out of gunnysacks. She devoted most of her time to feeding the goats and chickens that wandered at will in and out of Glenwood. Dick sank into depression. With his long hair and beard, he soon became the target of pranks by local children. One day, a group of rowdy boys chased him through the woods. Dick climbed up onto the roof of Glenwood and stayed there for two days without food or water. Afterward, Dick refused to admit to people that he was Dick Dana. People began referring to Dick as "Wild Man" and Octavia as "Goat Woman." Their once beautiful mansion became a dilapidated wreck. Curtains hung in tatters from the windows. Expensive rugs were stained and threadbare. Locals jokingly referred to the house as "Goat Castle."

Relations between Jennie Merrill and Dick and Octavia soon deteriorated. In 1917, Jennie attempted to purchase Glenwood by paying the delinquent taxes, but Octavia thwarted her scheme by having Dick declared legally insane. She was appointed Dick's legal guardian. As a result of her clever legal maneuvering, Dick could not be removed from his home because he was insane. The bad blood between the three people escalated in the late 1920s, when Jennie shot several goats that had been eating her rosebushes. The case went to trial, but charges were ultimately dropped.

On August 4, 1932, Dick Dana and Octavia Dockery were catapulted onto a list of suspects when Duncan rode out to Glenburnie for his nightly visit and discovered the front room in shambles. Blood was splattered on the walls. A trail of blood led out to the driveway. Duncan contacted the sheriff. All night, the sheriff and his posse combed the woods for Jennie Merrill. Sometime around dawn, they discovered her body hidden behind some bushes. She was barefoot and had been shot repeatedly by a .32-caliber pistol.

The next morning, Dick and Octavia were questioned; both were released a few days later. The lurid story was published in newspapers across the United States. Readers were enthralled by the photographs of the squalor in which Dick and Octavia lived. While Dick and Octavia were in jail, souvenir hunters plundered Glenwood. A few weeks later, Sheriff Roberts was notified by the police chief of Pine Bluff, Arkansas, that a man named George Pearls had been shot and killed by a policeman. Pearls had pulled a .32-caliber pistol on the policeman. Detectives soon uncovered Pearls's connection to Emily Burns, who ran a boardinghouse in Natchez. Emily later admitted that she and Pearls had tried to rob Jennie Merrill, but Jennie was shot when she tried to wrest the gun away from Pearls. Bloody fingerprints found at the scene matched those of Pearls. Emily Burns was later pardoned by the governor of Mississippi.

Aside from the damage wrought by vandals, Dick and Octavia actually benefited from their notoriety. They began charging people fifty cents a head to tour Goat Castle. On September 11, 1932, a train delivered six hundred people to Glenwood from Hattiesburg. Many more people came after that. Even though they were making money, Dick and Octavia neglected to pay the mortgage on the house. The mortgage holder tried to evict them, but Dick Dana died in 1948 of pneumonia and asthma before the case was settled. Octavia followed him in death in April 1949.

In his book *Dead Men Do Tell Tales*, author Troy Taylor recounts some of the ghost stories that began circulating around Natchez not long after Jennie Merrill's murder. Locals began avoiding the woods around Glenburnie at night because of the sightings of Jennie's ghost. People reported seeing a barefoot woman in a bloody blue dress running through the trees. Some people claimed that Dick Dana played the piano at night to drown out the moans and cries that echoed through the woods. After Dick and Octavia died, Octavia's ghost was seen wandering around the old house. Some people described her as an elderly lady wearing a calico dress. Others said they saw a lovely redheaded woman in a fine Paris gown inside the house. The eerie strains of Dick Dana's piano music were also heard resounding through the house.

Glenburnie itself was the subject of some of the ghost stories. When the old house was being restored in the 1980s, one of the owners said she heard a ghostly voice calling her name. She also said that every time an electrical cord was plugged in, invisible hands pulled it right back out again.

Glenwood is nothing more than a memory now. Octavia Dockery's cousins auctioned off the furnishings in the house soon after her death. The auction netted her family $15,000. In 1955, Glenwood was torn down to make room for a subdivision. Nothing remains of the old mansion but the strange stories of the wraith that is still sighted lurking in the woods near Glenburnie.

LONGWOOD

Haller Nutt was a wealthy businessman and planter, as well as a scientist and inventor. In 1864, he commissioned architect Samuel Sloan to design what would be the most unique house in Natchez. Dr. Nutt and Sloan envisioned an Oriental-style, octagonal mansion topped by a Byzantine Moorish dome and a twenty-four-foot finial. Construction on the doctor's townhouse began in 1860 but was halted in April 1861 after the Civil War broke out because the workers were needed in their militias back home. Today, the workmen's tools and scaffolds are in the same place the men dropped them so long ago.

By the time the workmen left, only the exterior of the six-story, thirty-thousand-square-foot mansion had been completed. Just nine of the fifty-two planned rooms were finished. Dr. Nutt, who did not really believe that a civil war would occur, had already spent $100,000 on his mansion.

He truly believed that the house would be finished in another six or eight months. He decided to make the nine rooms on the first floor habitable by installing windows, doors, woodwork and cypress floors.

His family moved into the first floor in 1862. Even though Dr. Nutt was a Federal sympathizer and had the papers to prove it, his plantations and steamboats were destroyed by the Union army. Dr. Nutt died of pneumonia on June 15, 1864, a broken man. He was forty-eight years old. In her diary. Dr. Nutt's wife, Julia, wrote that she and her husband had walked the galleries and dreamed a dream that never

Longwood.

The finished first floor.

was to be. She also wrote that after his death, she walked the galleries by herself. Julia and their eight children continued living on the first floor.

After the Civil War, Julia won her lawsuit against the U.S. government, but she still did not have enough money to put the finishing touches on her late husband's dream house. After her husband's death, Julia took on the task of raising and educating the children. In the next few decades, all of the eight remaining children grew up and moved away, with the exception of one unmarried daughter. Julia remained at Longwood for thirty-three years following her husband's death. She died on February 23, 1893, and was buried beside her husband and children in the family burying ground.

The last descendants of the Nutt family to live at Longwood were the five children of Lilly Nutt and her husband, James William Ward. In time, only an elderly grandson of Haller and Julia Nutt remained in the house. Soon, people began telling stories about seeing the ghost of

Longwood's unfinished floors.

Hall Nutt pacing inside the house and wandering through the grounds.

In her book *The Legend of Longwood*, author Margaret Shields Hendrix tells the story of an elderly handyman who was told to go inside Longwood and clean up the leaves and debris that had collected on the upper floors. In just a few minutes, he returned to the first floor, visibly shaken. He refused to return to the upper floors because he had seen a man in old clothes talking to himself.

In 1968, Mrs. Kelly E. McAdams of Austin, Texas, purchased Longwood from the three owners. In January 1970, she donated the home to the Pilgrimage Garden Club of Natchez. Longwood was formally dedicated as a National Historic Landmark on February 14, 1971. In Dr. Nutt's day, the people of Vicksburg called the unfinished mansion "Nutt's Folly." Today, it is known as the largest octagonal house in the United States. Longwood also has the reputation of being one of the most haunted houses in Natchez.

In her book *Ghosts! Personal Accounts of Modern Mississippi Hauntings*, author Sylvia Booth Hubbard says that a number of full-bodied apparitions have been sighted in Longwood over the years. In the 1980s, a grandson of Mrs. Louis Burns, the resident hostess at Longwood, was standing inside her room when he glanced over one of the chairs and was surprised to see a woman in a pink hoop skirt standing on the stairs. Perhaps Haller and Julia are still taking their melancholy strolls through their unfinished home.

I took a tour of Longwood on August 11, 2009. During our walk through this fascinating old house, the tour guide regaled my wife and me with stories about the paranormal activity inside the house. She said that when she started working here, she was told that if she made an unintentional error in her description of the mansion, the lights would blink off and on. However, if she intentionally gave the wrong date or the wrong name in her presentation, the lights would not blink. The tour guide said that the lights never turned off and on during her tours, so she assumes that she has always been telling the truth.

Our tour guide said that after she had been giving tours for a few weeks, when she opened up the house in the mornings, she discovered that somebody had been messing around during the night. "I can't tell you how many times we straightened up the portraits of Haller's mother and father in the master bedroom," she said. "When we come back to the house in the morning, they'll be crooked or turned sideways." The children's room is another active location inside the house. "Sometimes in the morning, the little children's furniture is scattered all over the place," our tour guide said. "I guess the ghost kids are playing with it." Longwood has a state-of-the-art alarm system and sprinkling system, so it is unlikely that someone has been breaking into the mansion during the night.

Although our tour guide told us that she has never felt frightened in Longwood, she has definitely had some unsettling experiences inside the mansion. "One afternoon,

I was in the rotunda, talking about the Nutt family. All of a sudden, I started getting goose bumps," she said. "It was in the middle of the summer, and the air conditioner wasn't on, so there is no logical reason why I should have gotten the chills." Our tour guide was convinced that she was in the presence of a spirit. For the most part, though, she is not really disturbed by the odd things that happen inside Longwood. "I just rock and roll with it," she laughed.

In 2010, tour guides at Longwood became even busier because of the publicity the magnificent old mansion received when it was selected as the home of Russell Edgington, the vampire king of Mississippi, for the third season of the HBO series *True Blood*.

NATCHEZ CITY CEMETERY

Natchez's old burying ground was located on a hill in what is now downtown Natchez, near Memorial Park and St. Mary's Cathedral. One of the people buried here was Samuel Brooks, who served as the first mayor of Natchez from 1803 to 1811. Mayor Brooks's casket is one of the few in the old burying ground that was not moved when Natchez City Cemetery was established in 1821 on the north side of the city, on a bluff overlooking the Mississippi River.

The city purchased the first part of the new cemetery—about ten acres—from Colonel John Steel for $1,000. Plots were sold for $15 apiece. The cemetery was divided up into one section for Roman Catholics, one section for strangers, one for persons of color and one for white people in general. Tombstones engraved with dates prior to 1800 mark the graves of bodies that were moved from the old burying ground and from churchyards and plantation graveyards. A number of prominent people are buried in Natchez City cemetery, including Don Jose Vidal, governor of Natchez Spanish District in 1798; General John A. Quitman, hero of the Mexican War; and Brigadier General Charles G. Dahlgren, commander of the Third Mississippi Regiment, CSA.

Natchez City Cemetery is renowned for its wrought-iron fences, decorative benches, iron mausoleum doors and beautiful marble monuments, most of which were created by Edwin Lyon and Robert Rawes. Natchez City Cemetery is also famous for its fascinating legends.

The most famous monument in the Natchez City Cemetery is the Turning Angel, which was erected to commemorate one of the city's worst catastrophes. On March 14, 1908, a terrible explosion completely destroyed the Natchez Drug Company at the corner of Main and South Union Street. The owner of the drug company bought a plot in the Natchez City Cemetery for the five girls who died in the explosion. The youngest girl was only twelve years old. He also paid for the monument of the grieving angel that was placed at the graveside. The inscription on the monument reads, "Erected by the Natchez Drug Company to the memory of the unfortunate employees who lost their lives in the great disaster that destroyed its building on March 14, 1908." The sculptor carved the statue in such a way that the face of the angel appears to turn toward visitors as they approach it. The

The Turning Angel monument in Natchez City Cemetery.

monument was made famous in a novel by Natchez native Greg Iles entitled *Turning Angel*.

Another unusual monument marks the grave of Rufus E. Case, who died at Wallenstein, Louisiana, on November 29, 1858. Case's monument resembles a wedding cake with its three tiers stacked one on top of the other. The story goes that Case was buried sitting up in his rocking chair not far from the grave of a child in his family who had preceded him in death.

Rufus Case's tomb.

The strangest grave in Natchez City Cemetery is that
of Florence Irene Ford, who was born on September 3,
1861. The child died of yellow fever at the age of ten on
October 30, 1871. Her mother, who was understandably
devastated by the death of her little girl, hated the thought
of being separated from her forever. She instructed the
workmen to construct steps of concrete leading six feet
down inside the grave. A specially installed glass pane
enabled her to look at her daughter's coffin. The story
goes that Florence hated thunderstorms when she was
alive, so when dark clouds appeared in the sky, her mother

This page: Florence Irene Ford's grave.

climbed down the steps and sat by her coffin until the storm dissipated.

Technically, Natchez City Cemetery is not a haunted site. The Turning Angel is probably nothing more than an optical illusion. Generations of children and teenagers have frightened one another by pretending to hear creaking sounds inside Rufus Case's monument or by claiming to have seen a bluish green light hovering over the grave of Florence Irene Ford. However, none of the stories that people have invented about Natchez City Cemetery are as intriguing as the truth.

NATCHEZ-UNDER-THE HILL

After Spain ceded Natchez and the surrounding area to the United States in 1798, Natchez became a supply city and the gateway to the West. In the late eighteenth century and early nineteenth century, Natchez-Under-the-Hill was known as one of the roughest, toughest landings on the Mississippi River. Between 1785 and 1820, flatboat men and other travelers headed home for Illinois, Indiana, Kentucky, Ohio and western Pennsylvania stopped off at Natchez-Under-the-Hill to drink, carouse and gamble before taking their chances on the Natchez Trace.

After flatboats were replaced by steamboats on the Mississippi River, thousands of people continued to whoop it up at this den of vice and corruption. In the town's heyday, as many as 150 boats were tied up at the wharves at one time. The three streets of Natchez-Under-the-Hill were about one mile long. They formed terraces running parallel with the Mississippi River. Water Street was bounded by the Mississippi River on one side and by a massive bluff on the other. The narrow street was dotted with a warehouse, wharves and shops built on stilt-like pilings. Many of these buildings were actually shacks constructed of planks from flatboats that had been dismantled on the shore not long after their arrival.

Behind Water Street was Middle or Royal Street. Situated above both streets was Silver Street, along which were located some of the more permanent structures, some of which were two or more stories high, like the Natchez Hotel and the Kentucky Tavern. Needless to say, the area's bars, brothels and gambling parlors attracted thousands of disreputable characters: thugs, murderers, prostitutes, drunks and tinhorn gamblers. Knife fights and shootouts were commonplace. This part of Natchez had such a bad reputation that in the 1840s and 1850s, scoundrels who were expelled from New Orleans sought refuge here, where even sheriffs and policemen feared to tread. Outlaws like the Harpe brothers—Micajah "Big" Harpe and Wylie "Little" Harpe—holed up here. Not surprisingly, the large number of deaths that occurred here has generated a number of colorful ghost stories.

The most commonly sighted ghost at Natchez-Under-the-Hill is the spirit of an outlaw named Joseph Thompson Hare. He was one of a host of brigands and murderers who robbed and killed merchants and settlers on the Natchez Trace in the early 1800s. Unlike most of the Natchez Trace

Natchez-Under-the-Hill.

criminals, Hare recounted his exploits in a journal, where he wrote about having a vision of a beautiful white horse. Hare believed that God sent him this vision as a warning to change his ways before it was too late. Hare ignored the vision and continued robbing and pillaging. Supposedly, he became involved with a woman of "low character." He plied her with diamonds and jewels taken from his victims in exchange for her loyalty while he was on one of his raids on the Natchez Trace. One day, he returned to Natchez convinced that his woman had entertained other men in his absence. According to one story, he weighted her down with rocks and jewels and buried her alive. Others say that he dumped her body in the Mississippi River. In 1818, Joseph Hare was arrested, tried and hanged. To this day, some people report hearing Joseph Hare's maniacal laughter as he watched his unfaithful lover's body float away.

Several other outlaws are said to haunt Natchez-Under-the-Hill. One of these men is John Murrel. He persuaded slaves to leave their plantations with the promise that he would help them escape to the North. Murrel ended up reselling the slaves at different plantations. Like Hare, Murrel was a highwayman who robbed and murdered unsuspecting travelers all over the South.

Three other outlaws are said to haunt Natchez-Under-the-Hill as well. Samuel Mason was called "the Wolfman" because of a front tooth that protruded from his lips. Two of his partners in crime sawed off his head to collect the reward money. One of these outlaws, Little Harpe, aroused the suspicion of the sheriff when he rode into town with a stolen horse. He was arrested and hanged by an angry mob. Little Harpe's brother, Big Harpe, was paralyzed by a bullet. He had boasted about killing a baby at King's Tavern because the infant was keeping him awake with its crying. The heads of all three of these outlaws were placed in trees along the Natchez Trace as a warning to other would-be criminals. The ghosts of all three outlaws have been seen walking the streets of Natchez-Under-the-Hill, apparently looking for liquor and women.

The other ghosts who stroll along Silver Street date back to the Spanish occupation of Natchez in the eighteenth century. Many people have seen a man in a military uniform who sold military secrets to the Spanish authorities. The ghosts of several Spanish soldiers have been seen as well.

Little remains of Natchez-Under-the-Hill today. The erosion of the riverbank and hillsides that began in 1797 eventually claimed more that 160 acres since the town was laid out. The New Madrid earthquake of 1811 created swollen currents and huge waves, which washed over many of the rickety buildings, causing them to tumble into the river. A number of buildings were crushed when a massive section of the bluff sheered off from the cliff face and plummeted to the town below.

By the 1830s, the planter elite of Natchez had become concerned about the racial mixing and the rumors of a slave revolt that was allegedly being planned at Natchez-Under-the-Hill. In November 1837, the planters issued an extralegal order: the pimps, whores and gamblers had twenty-four hours to clear out of Natchez. Overnight, hundreds of people moved from Natchez-Under-the-Hill to nearby New Orleans.

In 1840, a huge tornado blew down many of the dilapidated buildings along the river. Today, the little town that was once known as the "Barbary Coast of the Mississippi" is just a shadow of its former self. Only a few businesses that line Silver Street—the Silver Street,

Ltd., the River Boat Gift Shop, the Cock-of-the-Walk, the Under-the-Hill Saloon and the Natchez Landing—are still in operation. The area's unsavory reputation is kept alive in history books and in the ghost stories that tourists clamor to hear from the bartenders and shop owners.

THE EOLA HOTEL

The Eola Hotel was built by developer Isadore Levy, who named it after his daughter. When the seven-story hotel opened on July 1, 1927, it was praised by local newspapers as a symbol of the city's progress. In 1932, the Eola Hotel became the headquarters of Vicksburg's annual Natchez Pilgrimage Tour, attracting the rich and famous from all over the country. Unfortunately, the old hotel began to fall into disrepair in the 1960s.

The years of neglect finally took their toll in 1974, when the Eola Hotel closed. In 1978, the new owners began to restore the old landmark. The Eola was fully renovated at a cost of $6.5 million. Once again, guests marveled at the glistening chandeliers, the arched doorways, the marble trim and the famed Peacock Alley. In 1998, the Eola Hotel suffered a much more serious blow than the ravages of time. A tornado ripped off the roof and most of the top floor. Damages amounted to $30 million. Undaunted, the owners undertook an even more extensive restoration project. When the repairs were completed, the Eola Hotel was even more splendid than when it first opened. Today, the Eola Hotel is not only the tallest building in Natchez, but it is also the only hotel listed on the National Historic Register, due in large part to the attention the architect and the workmen paid to historic detail when the Eola was restored. Fittingly, the Eola Hotel is the command center for the annual antebellum home pilgrimages. It is also the most haunted hotel in Natchez.

The Eola Hotel is said to be haunted by Isadore Levy Eola, who died when she was sixteen years old. According to a story on Natchezontheriver.com, Patti Jenkins, who has worked at the Eola Hotel since 2002, said that several guests claim to have seen Eola's ghost. They described her as a teenage girl in a white dress. Patti said that she has frequently caught glimpses of human figures and heard spectral voices in her office. She is not certain that any of these apparitions was Eola. However, she does believe that she saw the ghost of the girl one day when she was running down the staircase to the hotel lobby, and she felt herself being nudged by an invisible presence. "She was telling me that it wasn't right," Patti said, "So I went over to the side and held the banister, and it didn't happen again." Patti believes that Eola's spirit was trying to tell her that she was not descending the stairs in a ladylike fashion. This theory does not explain why the food and beverage director was

The Eola Hotel.

violently shoved while running down the stairs one day. He tumbled head over heels and landed on the lobby floor. Miraculously, he escaped injury.

Eola's ghost might also have been seen by a woman who was painting the lobby before Christmas. She and her male co-worker had moved to an area near the front desk when a woman proceeded through the lobby in the direction of a door the pair had just painted. The man asked her not to exit through the door, but she ignored him and walked through it anyway. The female painter asked her co-worker who the girl was who had just walked through the door with the woman. He replied that the woman was totally alone. Patti Jenkins, who was working the front desk, said that she did not see a girl either. The female painter became so upset that she scooped up her equipment and rushed out the front door. She never again returned to the Eola Hotel.

Isadore Levy's ghost has appeared in the Eola Hotel as well. Late one night in 2001, when the bar was located on the seventh floor, the bartender was getting ready to close up when a nicely dressed man trolled over and ordered a drink. The bartender immediately sensed that something was wrong because the man was wearing a suit from the 1920s. She mixed the drink, and when she turned around to hand it to him, he was gone. A few minutes later, as she was getting ready to close up for the night, she was walking down the hallway when a portrait on the wall caught her eye. She returned to the portrait and was shocked to find herself staring at the likeness of the man she had just made a drink for. The picture was a portrait of Isadore Levy.

Most people are intrigued and even amused by the ghost stories told by the staff over the years. Not all guests think that the ghost stories are funny. Occasionally, guests have called down to the front desk in the middle of the night and asked to be moved to a different room. Patti Jenkins said that just before Christmas 2007, a lady who was attending a convention in town refused to turn off her lights during her entire four-day stay at the Eola Hotel because she believed that somebody was inside the room with her. The general manager of the Eola Hotel pooh-poohed the ghost stories until one day when he called the electricians to check out the wiring in a room where the lights were flickering. The electricians checked out the wiring for an hour and found nothing wrong. Apparently, it is difficult for people to stay—or work—at the Eola Hotel for an extended period of time without becoming believers in the paranormal.

KING'S TAVERN

Richard King, who hailed from New York, first settled in the Kingston area before moving to Natchez in the mid-eighteenth century. In 1789, Richard King bought King's Tavern, which had been built twenty years earlier. Sun-dried bricks, hand-hewn cypress clapboards and barge boards from flatboats that were dismantled and sold in Natchez were used in the construction of the inn, which resembles the blockhouses common to the American frontier. The timbers were fitted together with wooden pegs. The ground floor was originally used as a stable, with two smaller rooms where slaves lived. Cypress panels covered the walls on the main floor. The sleeping area on the second floor consisted of a small room and a larger room with a fireplace. In the 1820s, the east gallery was enclosed, thereby creating additional rooms. Travelers who were short on funds roomed in the attic, which had a floor made of cypress boards.

Richard King operated the building as a tavern from 1789 to 1820. The tavern also served as the first post office in Natchez. Indian runners delivered the mail to a small room. King's Tavern was a popular stop for weary travelers who had made their way to Natchez via the Natchez Trace. Richard King's clientele included politicians and soldiers, like Andrew Jackson and Aaron Burr, as well as murderous scoundrels, like the Harpe brothers. Bullet holes in the heavy wooden doors bear mute witnesses to the brawls that erupted fairly regularly.

In 1823, the Postlethwaite family purchased King's Tavern. The building continued to be used as a private residence until 1970. Since 1973, the building once again has been a combination tavern and restaurant. King's Tavern has become one of the city's most popular eateries. Its succulent steaks and impeccable service, as well as its status as the oldest building in Natchez, draw customers from within and outside of Natchez. In recent years, the restaurant's ghosts have been a big attraction as well.

Some of the ghosts that haunt King's Tavern are restless spirits who met a violent end here. One of these entities is the spirit of a beautiful sixteen-year-old girl named Madeleine, who was hired by the King family as a server. Richard soon became enamored of the girl and eventually seduced her. Richard's wife found out about Madeleine and disposed of her. Some people believe that the wife stabbed Madeleine and concealed her corpse behind the bricks in the chimney wall on the main floor. Others say

Above: King's Tavern.

Right: A portrait of
Madeleine above the
fireplace at King's Tavern.

that she hired a couple of thugs to do her dirty work. At any rate, Madeleine became a fading memory. Then, in the 1930s, workers who were enlarging the fireplace tore down the wall and made a grisly discovery. Hidden behind the wall were the skeletons of two men and one woman. Stuck between the ribs of the woman was a jeweled dagger. The find lent validity to the seemingly apocryphal tales that had been floating around Natchez for almost 150 years.

Legend has it that the ghost of the woman who has been seen in King's Tavern for many years is the spirit of

The fireplace and hearth at King's Tavern where three skeletons were found.

Richard King's young mistress, who cannot rest until her killer is brought to justice. Witnesses have described her as a lovely girl standing in a defiant stance with her hands on her hips. In an interview with Sheila Turnage, author of *Haunted Inns of the Southeast*, owner Yvonne Scott said that her daughter saw the ghostly figure of a woman standing in front of the fireplace. Yvonne also said that one day, she and a visitor were sitting at a table in the main dining room. When the visitor began asking questions about Madeleine, an antique chain hanging on the wall began swinging back and forth. Many patrons swear that they have seen her portrait hanging over the fireplace in the main dining room swing back and forth on occasion.

The staff at King's Tavern attributes many of the strange, unexplained occurrences to Madeleine's spirit. She has been blamed for opening doors. If the staff member says, "All right, Madeleine!" the doors shut by themselves. One night, at closing time, the last two employees to leave the tavern turned off the lights and locked the door. They were walking to their cars when they noticed that all of the lights were back on. By the time they unlocked the door and walked inside, the lights were back off.

Jars have been flung off shelves by an unseen hand. Madeleine's ghost also likes to play with water, apparently. Sonja Frost, an employee at King's Tavern, told author Sheila Turnage that puddles of water mysteriously appear on the second floor. At times, guests walking around on the second floor have felt water dripping on their heads. When they move to a different spot, more drops of water fall from the ceiling. Hot water has been known to come out of pipes without a hot water line. When the tavern first opened, employees were shocked to find hot water coming out of a dead pipe. Wet footprints, the size of a woman's foot, have appeared on freshly mopped floors.

A waitress who had been working at King's Tavern for only a year had an alarming number of weird experiences in the old restaurant:

> *I had lights turn off on me when I was in one of the dining rooms on the ground floor. Water dripped on my head in an area where there were no pipes. I have had straws thrown at me. Something has unfolded napkins on the tables. I have arranged place settings and when I came back a few minutes later, the forks have been scattered across the table.*

The young woman's most terrifying experience occurred one night when she was locking up for the night:

> *I was getting ready to leave when I decided to go to the restroom. While I was in the restroom, I heard someone lock the door from the outside. I had to call my boss to come to the tavern and unlock the door. I know that I was the only one inside King's Tavern at the time. This is the reason why there are no locks on the bathroom doors.*

One of the most terrifying encounters with Madeleine's spirit occurred in 1974. A tour guide in one of the city's antebellum homes said that when her daughter was in the ninth grade, she was selling Christmas cards to raise money for her school's drill team. Late one afternoon, her mother drove the girl to King's Tavern to meet with a member of the staff who had expressed an interest in buying some of the cards. To her daughter's dismay, the door was locked. She walked around the building, looking through windows for the person who was supposed to talk to her. All at once, the girl dashed to the car and said, "Let's go!" After they arrived home, her daughter said that while she was looking through one of the windows, she saw a woman in a red riding suit walk down the stairs. She was wearing boots and a hat. Her daughter said that the figure was dressed like women who participate in equestrian shows. The girl stared at the woman for just a few seconds before the apparition vanished.

Another ghost story has its roots in the most heinous crime committed in the old tavern. The story goes that in the late 1700s, a woman was trying to calm down her screaming infant in the mailroom, which is now the Tap Room. After a few minutes, the door to the adjoining room slowly opened, and a huge, bearded man stumbled into the mailroom. He approached the woman and asked her if he could have the baby. The woman assumed that the man was going to help her quiet down her daughter, so she gratefully placed the child in his arms. As the woman stared in horror,

Madeleine's ghost has been seen descending these steps at King's Tavern.

the man grabbed the infant by the ankles and slammed her head against the wall. He then returned the battered little body to her weeping mother and went back to bed. The heartless fiend was Big Harpe, a notorious outlaw, who, with his brother Little Harpe, terrorized travelers on the Natchez Trace.

Yvonne Scott said that staff and patrons have often heard the cries of a baby coming from the attic. One day, she was sitting at her desk in the kitchen when she heard the unmistakable sound of a baby crying. She turned to the cook and a waitress and asked, "What's that?" Both women verified that Yvonne had heard the cries of a baby. They searched the entire tavern but found no sign of a baby. In an interview in 2001, Danny Scott, Yvonne Scott's daughter, told me, "Sometimes when I'm up there, I have trouble catching my breath, like I'm being suffocated. Then, after I've been up there, I'll hear the baby crying for days afterwards, like it's reaching out for help."

Little is known about two of the tavern's other ghosts. One of them is the ghost of an Indian, probably one of the runners who delivered mail to King's Tavern in the late eighteenth and early nineteenth centuries. He is usually seen in the Tap Room standing in front of the window facing the street. Danny Scott said that his ghost also frequently appears at midnight in front of the fireplace of the old mailroom. The Indian has been described as wearing a full war bonnet.

An even stranger spirit in King's Tavern is the apparition of a man with a top hat. Several patrons have captured the image of a man wearing a dark jacket, pants, a black string tie and a top hat in photographs taken by the fireplace in the main dining room. A few people have felt an invisible hand on their shoulders and neck. His appearance often evokes fear in those who see him, leading to the belief that he might be the ghost of one of the outlaws who preyed on boatmen or sojourners on the Natchez Trace.

In 2001, I spent the night in King's Tavern, along with Scotty Ray Boyd and Debbie Alexander, two disc jockeys

The Tap Room at King's Tavern where the Indian's ghost has been seen.

from a Meridian radio station, and a reporter from the *Meridian Star*. The waitress who was giving us a tour of King's Tavern took us up to the guest suite on the third floor. She told us that sometimes people see the image of a man in the mirror out of the corners of their eyes. The waitress also said that sometimes, when people run their hands a few inches above the bed, they feel the warmth of a human body. Later, everyone in our group tried unsuccessfully to detect hot spots on the old bed.

The bedroom on the second floor at King's Tavern.

The impression of a bear's paw at the entrance to King's Tavern.

On August 12, 2009, I returned to King's Tavern with my wife, Marilyn. After showing her the impression of a panther's and a bear's paw in the entranceway, we were seated in a table next to the chain that reportedly moves on its own. Both of us took a number of photographs with our digital cameras in the hopes of catching orbs or mists. Nothing unusual showed up in our photographs, so we resumed our meal. After a few minutes, Marilyn told me that she was feeling dizzy. Marilyn has demonstrated sensitivity to paranormal activity on several occasions, so I suggested that we step outside for a few minutes. Marilyn felt better as soon as we walked out the front door. Five minutes later, we returned to our table. Marilyn's bout of dizziness did not return for the remainder of our meal.

Like many haunted places that depend on the patronage of the public, King's Tavern publicizes its ghost stories. In fact, when I visited King's Tavern in 2009, I purchased a photocopy of an article published years ago in the *National Enquirer* about author Sylvia Booth Hubbard's unsettling experiences inside the old tavern, including the chains that swung from the wall when her husband was taking her photograph. However, King's Tavern stands out among haunted restaurants and hotels in that most of the time, the employees find it difficult to laugh off the strange incidents that occur on a regular basis. The testimony of the owners and the staff clearly suggests that working at King's Tavern can, at times, be quite frightening.

LINDEN

The earliest part of Linden was built in 1790. The east wing was added in 1818. Further additions were made in 1829 and 1850. One of the earliest owners of Linden was Senator Thomas Reed. In 1849, Linden was purchased by William and Jane Conner. Today, Linden is owned by Jeanette Feltus. Her family is the sixth generation to live in the old house.

For many years, Linden has been a regular stop on the Natchez Pilgrimage Tour. Today, Linden is one of the city's most popular bed-and-breakfasts. Movie buffs have traveled to Linden just to see the front door, which set designers copied for the movie *Gone with the Wind*. The old mansion is recognized far and wide for its beauty, its southern hospitality and its ghost stories.

Linden has been known as a haunted house for generations. In an interview conducted by Sylvia Booth

The door at Linden served as the model for the front entranceway in Tara in the film *Gone with the Wind*.

Hubbard for her book *Ghosts!*, Jeanette Feltus said that one afternoon around the turn of the century, family members were sitting on the back gallery. Suddenly, they heard the crunching sound of the wheels of a buggy on the gravel road that wound around Linden. They recognized the sound of the wheels, but they were bewildered because they realized that the owner of the buggy had died a few days before. A male member of the family ran to the front of the house. Within a few minutes, he reported back to the others that no one was there.

Many years later, when Jeanette's husband, Richard, was a boy, he saw an entirely different ghost. One afternoon,

Linden.

he and several of his friends were playing pool upstairs. He was trying to take a shot when one of the boys ran into the room and told the others to look out the window. Richard was stunned by what he saw. A woman jumped off the roof and floated across the courtyard. She disappeared before she landed on the ground.

Jeanette said that when her father-in-law, Dick Feltus, was living at Linden, he was sleeping in the bedroom on the first floor when he was awakened by the feeling that he was being watched. Rubbing the sleep from his eyes, he was amazed to see his cousin, who had died a few days before, standing at the foot of the bed. Dick asked his cousin how he was doing. His cousin replied that he was fine and that he had just come back to see how everyone was doing. Dick, who had been close to his cousin, tried to shake his cousin's hand, but the young man shook his head and vanished.

After his death in the late 1970s, Richard Conner Feltus became the most commonly sighted ghost at Linden. "My father-in-law was the fourth generation of Conners to live in Linden," Jeanette said.

> *When he was elderly, he had several strokes, and he had to walk with a cane. He loved milk punch, but he could no longer drink it out of a cup, so we had to put it in a Pepsi Cola bottle so he could drink it. He had a little refrigerator in his bedroom where he'd keep it. Some nights when Dick couldn't sleep, you could hear him in the middle of the night going "peck, peck, peck" with his cane out on the gallery. He'd sit down in one of the chairs and have a drink or two of his milk. Then he'd go "peck-peck-peck" back to his room. Every now and then, guests staying in Dick's Room hear the tapping of his cane out on the gallery.*

Several years ago, three couples who had rented rooms in the gallery where Dick had spent so many sleepless nights reported hearing somebody walking around all night with a cane. It turned out that they had heard Dick's ghost on his birthday.

Linden

Above: The gallery at Linden where Dick Feltus drank his milk punch.

Right: Dick's cane hanging by the front door at Linden.

Jeanette says that one couple who stayed in Dick's Room had a humorous encounter with his ghost:

> *Several years ago, I had a couple come to Linden. They were on their second marriage. Each of their spouses had died. We were at the breakfast table, and the husband said, "My wife tossed and turned all night long." I said, "Oh, was there something wrong with the mattress?" And he said, "Oh, no. I woke up, and there at the foot of the bed were two gentlemen, a lady, and two children." I said, "I can tell you who they were. They were Murrell, my father-in-law's brother; Dick, my father-in-law; Dick's sister, Margaret; and two of Margaret's children." The man's wife asked, "Where are they?" I said, "They're dead." The husband said, "I figured that because they all left but one, and he got in bed with us." I said, "That was Dick, but you don't have to worry. He's a perfect gentleman."*

In 2005, a different couple encountered one of Linden's other ghosts in Margaret's Room on the second floor of the main house. "The couple came with their daughter," Jeanette said.

> *She was very talented. She had a beautiful voice and played piano. The father woke up in the middle of the night because he heard somebody singing. So he woke up his wife and said, "What is Caroline doing? Singing*

in her sleep?" His wife said, "That is not Caroline singing." They both heard somebody singing in the house. We don't know who it was because neither the Connors nor the Feltuses could carry a tune in a bucket.

Down through the years, Jeanette's family members have experienced visits from ghosts that have not been identified. The ghost of a man wearing a top hat has appeared in one of her daughter's bedroom on several occasions. "Both of my daughters lived upstairs," Jeanette said.

Each room had two beds, so when they had company, they had a bed for them. A lot of these girls came down the next morning and said, "Ms. Feltus, you know how you feel when someone's staring at you? I woke up, and there was a man standing by my bed with a top hat on." I always said, "Oh, that's cousin John. He lives in the attic." When I just moved in the house, I could hear him stomping in the attic. He's sort of quieted down now. I guess he's gotten used to me. Anyway, I always told Cousin John if he'd just stay up in the attic, I'd stay down here. I had a guest once who offered to hold a séance and send him to heaven. I said I didn't want to do that because he keeps me safe.

In 2010, a woman who had booked Dick's Room was getting ready for bed when the door opened several times by itself. After she was convinced that whatever was causing the disturbance had stopped for the night, she turned off the lights and went to sleep. Just past midnight, she heard the heavy footsteps of someone walking through the room. After about a minute, the walking stopped. Then she heard a deep male voice whisper in her ear, "I'm sorry I bothered you." The next morning, the woman reported the strange incident to Jeanette, who simply said, "That was Dick's voice you heard. He's a very polite ghost."

On June 13, 2010, I spent a peaceful night in Dick's Room, totally undisturbed by the tapping sound that so many guests have heard coming from the gallery. Feeling

Dick's Room in Linden where Dick kept his refrigerator.

disappointed at not encountering Dick's ghost, my wife and I went to breakfast the next morning in the dining room. After we finished our meal of scrambled eggs, ham, grits, biscuits and fruit, we and the other guests were entertained by Ms. Feltus's explanation of the antique furnishings inside the dining room. During her presentation, my wife and I clearly heard a clicking sound behind us. We turned around and noticed that one of the two identical three-tier china servers sitting on top of the sideboard was shaking. Marilyn and I found it difficult to concentrate on Jeanette's presentation until the clicking finally stopped two minutes later.

In recent years, several of her guests have collected evidence of the existence of the ghosts at Linden, including Jeanette's favorite ghost, Dick. "When Dick died," she said, "we hung his cane on the hall tree in the front hallway. About a month or so ago, a houseguest took a picture of the cane. She sent me a copy of it. You can see the aura swirling around the cane." Jeanette said that the lady's camera also captured the image of a man by the door, but she hasn't sent it yet. Actually, the ghosts at Linden have been so successful at making their presence known over the years that photographic evidence seems to be unnecessary.

MONMOUTH

Postmaster John Hankinson built the Federal-style mansion that became Monmouth in 1818 on the outskirts of Natchez, where some of the finest homes in the city were located. Hankinson named the house after the place of his birth, Monmouth County, New Jersey. The estate also consisted of a one-story, two-room dependency that housed the kitchen. John Hankinson lived at Monmouth with his wife, Francis, and their six children until 1823, when financial setbacks forced him to mortgage the main house and thirty-four acres. Hankinson defaulted on the loan, so the estate was sold at auction to Calvin Smith. John Hankinson died before the sale was completed, and his wife died a few years later. Both John and Francis Hankinson are buried on the Monmouth estate.

The next owner of Monmouth was John Anthony Quitman. Born in New York in 1799, Quitman, who had always aspired to live the life of a gentleman, moved to Natchez in 1821 with the intention of becoming a lawyer. He soon set up a lucrative law practice in partnership with John McMurran. Eventually, Quitman joined the Masons and became president of a railroad and a bank. He was also director of a steamboat company. Quitman married Eliza Turner, the daughter of one of the city's most prominent families. In 1826, he purchased Monmouth from Calvin Smith for $12,000. In 1842, Quitman built a greenhouse on his property. Several years later, he added a brick barn and stable.

In the 1850s, John and Eliza made radical alterations to Monmouth. They replaced some of the first-floor mantelpieces with white- and beige-veined black marble. They also changed the front of the house to the Greek Revival style. They covered up the outside brick with stucco as well. They then began construction on the east wing, which was attached to the house by a rear gallery. The lower level was taken up with John's library; the upper floor was used for family and guests. The kitchen and carriage house occupied the first floor of a brick building in the rear of the main house. Slaves were housed on the upper floor. The grounds were embellished with beautiful gardens, flower beds and orchids. A peach tree sent to Quitman by his brother became the first of many fruit trees that he planted at Monmouth. He planted a number of other trees as well, including pecans, oaks, redbuds and pines.

Monmouth.

In the mid-nineteenth century, the Quitmans entertained some of the South's wealthiest and most powerful figures, although they rarely gave formal parties. Jefferson Davis was a guest at Monmouth. Henry Clay received the gift of a magnolia tree while visiting Manmouth. For the most part, though, the Quitmans arranged informal gatherings for their friends and relatives. Even though John and Eliza had eleven children, Monmouth was, at times, a "dismal and barren place," as his daughter Antonia described it in a letter. Eventually, Eliza did entertain more guests, most of whom were John's military buddies from the Mexican War.

In 1863, during the Texas Revolution, Quitman responded to Sam Houston's plea for volunteers. He commanded a small company of volunteer Mississippians, who joined up with Sam Houston after the Battle of San Jacinto. Within a year, Quitman led a combined force of volunteers, regulars and U.S. Marines in an attack against Chapultepec Castle. They then besieged the gates of Mexico City. After the surrender of the defenders of the city, Major General Winfield Scott appointed Quitman governor of the capital of Mexico.

Quitman's distinguished military service opened the door to a splendid career in politics. He served in Congress and was elected to two terms as governor of Mississippi. By the time Quitman died on July 17, 1857, he owned four corn and sugar plantations in Mississippi and Louisiana. He had apparently contracted an illness similar to Legionnaires' disease known at the time as National Hotel disease after speaking to President James Buchanan at the National Hotel in Washington, D.C. He was buried on the grounds of Monmouth, but within a few years, his remains, as well as the remains of his family, were reinterred at the Natchez City Cemetery.

Monmouth, like other antebellum homes in Natchez, felt the impact of the Civil War. When the Union army occupied Natchez in May 1863, the Quitman family's slaves fled the plantation. Union officers took up residence in Monmouth. Meanwhile, Quitman's daughters and their families had to live upstairs. A few of the Quitmans' slaves returned to Monmouth on the condition that they be paid for their services. Before the Civil War ended in 1865, soldiers from the Fifty-eighth United States Colored Infantry camped on Monmouth's lawn and helped themselves to the family's fruit and produce. After the Civil War, poverty compelled the Quitmans to sell their furniture, clothing, carpets and personal possessions. Ironically, Monmouth was saved from destruction by a Union general, Henry W. Slocum, who had befriended the Quitman family. The Quitmans were forced to take an oath of loyalty to the United States. Years later, John Quitman's descendants sued the United States government for damages incurred during the Civil War.

Times were equally hard for the Quitman family during Reconstruction. Members of the Quitman family continued living in Monmouth until 1875, when other families rented out the main house and grounds. Most of the acreage was converted to the growing of cotton. In 1889, members of the Quitman family once again took over the family home. In 1884, John Quitman's daughter, Annie Rosalie, had bought Monmouth from her sisters, Louisa and Fredericka. In 1888, Annie Rosalie began replanting the shrubs, flowers and trees that had once adorned the grounds of Monmouth. During this time, Louisa's daughters, Eva and Alice, moved in with Aunt Rosalie. They were joined by descendants of Monmouth's slaves, who continued to work as paid servants for forty-five years after the Civil War.

In 1919, Monmouth was sold to people outside of the Quitman family. In 1922, Natchez widow Annie Gwin took possession of Monmouth. She married Herbert Barnum, who transformed Monmouth into a dairy farm. Members of Barnum's family continued to own and live at Monmouth for over fifty years. Because of the renewed interest in the Old South in the 1930s, Monmouth was included on the Natchez Pilgrimage Tour of homes, even though it had deteriorated greatly since it was first built in 1818.

Following Annie Barnum's death in 1960, her children put the old plantation up for sale. No buyers came forth, so Monmouth continued to decline until a couple from California, Ronald Riches and his wife, Lani, discovered the old house. They purchased it in 1978 and immediately began restoring it. They hired local contractors and businessmen to garner community support for their project. A local contractor named Danny Smith, who did all of the carpentry, won praise from the Mississippi Department of Archives and History for the attention he paid to historical detail. Natchez interior designer and antique dealer Buzz Harper assisted with landscaping and interior design. The restorers utilized a map created by Union army engineers as a guide for the original location of antebellum driveways, trees and buildings no longer in existence. Landscape architect William Garbo Sr. created a pre–Civil War garden. The Riches also preserved a terraced area in the back of the property.

Today, Monmouth is operated as a bed-and-breakfast. It has also become a popular venue for weddings. Movies and television shows have been filmed on the grounds. Recently, people interested in the paranormal have converged on Monmouth in search of the ghosts that are said to reside here.

In many haunted houses, the most active ghost is the spirit of an inhabitant with a dominant personality. Not surprisingly, John Anthony Quitman is the most commonly sighted ghost at Monmouth. He was first detected in the late 1970s, when Lani and Ron Riches began restoring the old house. Workers reported feeling as though they were being watched by what they described as a "strong presence." After the Richeses moved their family into the old home, their daughters, who were little girls at the time, said that when they were sleeping in Room 23, they heard someone stomping up the stairs. They told their parents that it sounded like someone wearing boots with leather soles was walking up wooden stairs. Their experience was especially disturbing because the entire house, including the stairs, was carpeted.

In the next few years, everyone in the family heard the stomping, except for Lani Riches. Even the staff, workmen and police claimed to have heard someone clomping around the house at all hours. A little later, the girls were getting ready to sleep when they saw a man walk through the room and vanish into the opposite wall. A few months later, a guest staying in Room 30 saw a man wearing a blue military uniform walk toward his bed. The guest was struck by the fact that the strange figure's boots made a clicking sound on the floor. The ghost looked around the room and then disappeared.

In 1989, a man and his wife saw a male ghost from a later era. They said that they were walking on the sidewalk

The gardens at Monmouth.

at the rear of the main house in the direction of the gift shop when they saw a man wearing a Confederate uniform walk out of the rose garden and head across the courtyard. The closer he got to the buildings, the more transparent he became. He had not taken more than fifty steps before he completely dissipated.

Some unidentified entities have also made their presences known at Monmouth. One of the gardeners said that on nights when he worked late, he has walked inside Monmouth and heard weird noises coming from the attic. One of the ladies who work in the gift shop said that one afternoon, a lady who had taken a walk around the gardens in the back returned to the gift shop looking very distressed. Wiping a tear from her eye, she said that she saw a lady and a child crying by the pond. The woman, who said she was a medium, sensed that the lady and the child were crying because a baby had just died. The lady in the gift shop informed the woman that Mrs. Quitman had eleven children, only six of whom grew to adulthood. The sensitive guest had most likely seen Mrs. Quitman's ghost and the ghost of one of her children.

The pond at Monmouth.

Several years ago, the office manager was leaving the main house one night. She turned on the burglar alarm and noticed that the message "Disturbance in Zone 4" came up. She walked into the parlor and was startled by the sight of the prisms hanging from a lamp swinging back and forth. She was dumbstruck at first. Then, a few seconds later, she realized that she was in the presence of something very weird. She stopped the prisms from moving and went back to the other room. The woman turned off the alarm and returned to the parlor. Once again, the prisms were moving on their own. After she stopped the prisms, she looked up toward the ceiling and announced, "That will be enough of that! I don't want to have to come back in here!" The office manager continued talking to the mischievous spirit all the way back through the house.

A few years after the Riches moved into Monmouth, they had a clergyman come into the house and say a blessing in every room in the main house. Since then, the general's "heavy walking" has ceased. Nevertheless, the people who live and work at Monmouth find comfort in the feeling that General John Anthony Quitman approves of the changes they made to his beloved home and that he is watching over them.

THE OLD ADAMS COUNTY JAIL

The grim-looking Victorian building at 314 State Street is the Adams County Supervisor's Office. Between 1891 and 1975, however, it housed the Adams County Jail. On the top floor are four iron cells that face an open area. These heavy jail cells constituted Death Row. In the middle of the ceiling is an ominous-looking iron ring. Criminals convicted of capital crimes stood on top of a trapdoor underneath the iron ring. One end of the rope was tied around the ring, and the other end was tied around their necks. When the signal was given by the sheriff, a jailer pulled a large lever, and the convicts fell through the trapdoor to their deaths.

Many people were executed in the Old County Jail until 1936, when the last hanging took place there. The lever operating the trapdoor is still present. After the new jail was constructed next door in 1975, the old Adams County

The Old County Jail.

Jail stood empty for several years until it became the Adams County Supervisor's Office. According to testimony given by former jail employees, employees in the Adams County Supervisor's Office and by the convicts themselves, the Old County Jail is the most haunted building in Natchez.

Former sheriff Tommy Ferrell had a lot to say about the ghosts in the Old Adams County Jail in an interview published on Natchezontheriver.com. Ferrell, whose father was also sheriff of Adams County, played in the jail as a child and knows more about the ghost stories than anyone in Vicksburg. Ferrell said that for many years, prisoners complained about hearing moaning, walking and the dragging of chains at all hours. They also said they heard jail cells open and close when none of the jailers or policemen was present. One prisoner even claimed to have been asleep in his cell when he awoke to find a heavy iron chain wrapped around his neck. He yelled at the top of his lungs while trying to extricate himself from the chain. By the time help arrived, he had freed himself.

Jailers and trustees who lived at the jail had experiences that substantiated the claims made by the prisoners. Ferrell recalled a group of trustees who were standing on ladders, painting the ceiling. When prisoners approached the trapdoor, they began hearing voices. Ferrell said that the trustees were so upset by what they had heard that they did not want to live in the jail anymore. The disturbances in the jail were so common, in fact, that a number of jailers refused to live there. Ferrell said that a deputy who was on dispatch duty by himself in the jail one night discovered that there was truth in the stories he had heard from the other people who worked there. He walked into the kitchen to make a sandwich and was amazed to see a loaf of bread floating in the air. By the time he had pulled his gun from his holster, the bread was back on the counter. The deputy never went back in the kitchen again.

Employees in the Adams County Supervisor's Office have also encountered the ghosts in the Old Adams County Jail. A secretary and inventory clerk named Angela Hutchins worked in the building for several years. One night, she was standing in the hallway when she saw someone in a red shirt walk into the conference room. She walked into the room, and no one was there. A few minutes later, he showed up in the same room once again. She checked to see if the intruder had gone out the back door, but it was still locked from the inside. As a feeling of dread swept over her, Angela recalled the other strange things that occurred on a regular basis inside the former jail, such as the stairs that seemed to creak on their own and the telephones that lit up when no one was on the other end of the line.

Most experts in the paranormal believe that the majority of ghosts are harmless. They are the residual energy of people who have died and have not yet crossed over to the other side. The ghosts in the Old Adams County Jail are a different breed altogether. "We were concerned with the nature of the people being dealt with in the jail," Ferrell said. "We didn't know if there were going to be more confrontations [than with the ghosts found in the antebellum houses in town]."

STANTON HALL

Frederick Stanton was born near Belfast, Ireland, on February 16, 1794. He immigrated to America when he was twenty-one years old. Stanton eventually moved to Natchez, where he met his future wife, Hulda Laura Helm. They were married on July 3, 1827. Over the next few years, the Stantons lived at two lavish homes in Vicksburg: Cherokee and Glenwood. By the late 1840s, Stanton had made a fortune as a cotton planter and as the senior partner of the commission house of Stanton, Buckner and Company of New Orleans and Natchez. In 1849, Stanton was ready to build a house that was worthy of one of the richest men in Adams County. On May 12, 1849, Stanton purchased a plot of land bordered by High, Pearl, Commerce and Monroe Streets. He hired architect Captain Thomas Rose, who hired local artisans and workmen. Rose completed the mansion Stanton called Belfast in 1858 at

Stanton Hall.

a cost of $83,262.23. Historians believe that Rose might have used Stanton's ancestral home at Belfast as a model for Stanton Hall.

When the Stanton family moved into Stanton Hall in 1858, the mansion exceeded the expectations of the citizens of Vicksburg. An article in the *Mississippi Free Trader* described the Stanton residence as "magnificent and princely." Frederick Stanton planted a number of oak trees, many of which are still standing. The house was constructed of clay bricks that were burned on the premises. The bricks were then covered over with stucco and painted white.

The imposing front door was flanked with four huge white Corinthian columns. The entranceway led into an arched hall seventy-two feet long. Not only were the doorknobs made of Sheffield silver, but so were the lock plates, hinges and call bells. The interior of the mansion reflects the Greek Revival and Italianate styles. Gold mirrors and bronze chandeliers were hung in the front and rear parlors. The gold leaf mirrors were made in France. The five first-floor fireplace mantels were carved from the finest white Carrara marble. The mantels were sculptured in New York.

Frederick Stanton did not live very long in his palatial home. He died a month after the home was completed in 1858. During the Siege of Vicksburg, the Stanton home was slightly damaged by a gunboat's cannonball. The story goes that when a company of privates occupied Belfast, they chloroformed Elizabeth Stanton and her daughter, Vanna. While the women were sleeping, the soldiers stole several pieces of silver hidden underneath the bed. After Elizabeth Stanton died in 1893, her relatives took or sold many of the furnishings in the house. Between 1894 and 1901, Belfast housed Stanton College for Young Ladies. The main building was connected by a covered walkway to a covered walkway that was built between 1892 and 1897. In 1901, the porte-cochère was added to the west side of the house, which was renamed Stanton Hall. That same year, Stanton College was relocated to the Kelly house, Choctaw.

Mr. and Mrs. A.G. Campbell, the next private owners of the mansion, shortened the rear wing and added a garage at the center of the rear property line. Stanton Hall was then purchased by Mr. and Mrs. Clark, who lived in the house until it was purchased by the Pilgrimage Garden Club in 1938. By this time, the house was almost entirely empty, so the Pilgrimage Garden Club decided to acquire period furnishings by means of loans and gifts. In the 1940s, the Pilgrimage Garden Club held a number of fundraising events to pay for the renovation of Stanton Hall. During World War II, soldiers from Camp Van Dorn attended dances at Stanton Hall. Bedrooms were rented out to guests at this time, as well. Until 1992, Stanton Hall was operated as a bed-and-breakfast. Down through the years, the club has continued to raise money by offering tours of the house and by hosting receptions and parties at Stanton Hall.

In her book *Ghosts! Personal Accounts of Modern Mississippi Hauntings*, author Sylvia Booth Hubbard tells of the experience Mrs. Vera Daimwood, retired associate manager of the Mississippi Tourism Department, had at Stanton Hall during the Natchez Mardi Gras. Mrs. Daimwood and Mississippi's Miss Hospitality were spending the night at Stanton Hall. Mrs. Poole, the housekeeper, told them to call her before they left the reception that evening so that she could turn off the alarm system. Once Mrs. Daimwood and Miss Hospitality had entered the mansion through the front door, Mrs. Poole would reset the alarm. She also told them to be out of the mansion by 9:00 a.m., before the tours began.

The next morning, Mrs. Daimwood was lying in bed when she heard a man's deep voice say, "Good morning."

She sat up and looked around. Seeing no one in the room, she fell back asleep. A few minutes later, she again heard the deep voice. Still groggy, she looked over at the alarm clock. The time was 6:00 a.m. Mrs. Daimwood assumed that she had heard the voice of the yardman. At 7:00 a.m., Mrs. Daimwood woke up Miss Hospitality and went down to breakfast. Mrs. Poole, who was working in the kitchen, asked Mrs. Daimwood how she had slept. Mrs. Daimwood said that she slept fine but that the yardman woke her up at sunrise. With a puzzled expression on her face, Mrs. Poole replied that there were no yardmen at Stanton Hall. They had done all of their work the day before. Smiling, she informed Mrs. Daimwood that she should feel privileged because Colonel Stanton's ghost does not talk to everybody. Mrs. Poole went on to say that sometimes the ghosts of the Stanton family rattle her doorknob and wake her up. She added that sometimes she hears the "patter of little feet" in the hallway, most likely the footsteps of the ghosts of the Stantons' children.

Today, the alarm system goes off at least once a month, even though no one actually lives in the house. Electricians have found nothing wrong with the wiring or the sensors placed around the house.

The most commonly reported ghost in Stanton Hall is connected to the youngest members of the families who have owned the house. In the 1870s and 1880s, the Stanton family owned a black cocker spaniel. Frederick and Hulda's children and grandchildren were so fond of the little dog that it was treated like a member of the family. Apparently, the pooch felt so welcome in Stanton Hall that it never really left, even after it died. When I toured Stanton Hall on August 12, 2009, one of the tour guides told me:

> *People touring the house tell us that they have seen a little black cocker spaniel inside the house. We laugh about the little ghost. We blame him if we hear creaks or squeaks. Of course, you hear creaks and squeaks all the time in old houses, so the dog's ghost might not be responsible.*

Proof of the cocker spaniel's existence surfaced in 1946, when a portrait of Frederick Stanton and a small black dog was returned to the mansion.

Today, Stanton Hall is much more than just a historic home. It serves as the headquarters of the Pilgrimage Garden Club. It is also a popular venue for wedding receptions and other elegant social functions. Each year, the Carriage House Restaurant and Lounge attracts hundreds of visitors eager to sample authentic southern fare, such as southern fried chicken and mint juleps. The Gay Nineties building next door to the restaurant houses the club's offices. The loving care lavished on the fine old mansion by the volunteers is evident everywhere. Apparently, the love for the family dog has preserved its spirit as well.

SPRINGFIELD

Springfield is the oldest plantation in the Natchez area. The two-story mansion was built between 1786 and 1791 by Thomas Marston Green, a planter from Virginia. It was the first full-columned mansion to be built west of the Atlantic seaboard. The bricks used in the construction of the house were fired on the plantation in wood-fired kilns. Green's slaves also cut down the trees and fashioned the timbers and boards that went into the construction of the house. The hinges for the windows and doors were made in a blacksmith shop at Springfield. The interior of the plantation house was embellished with hand-carved mantels and Georgian-Adam-Federal woodwork. Unlike many plantation houses at that time, Springfield's entry room does not have a formal staircase. Instead, an enclosed staircase leads up to a single guest room.

Springfield.

Springfield Plantation is remembered today because of a marriage that is alleged to have taken place there in 1790. According to one version of the story, Rachel Donelson was sent to Natchez by her mother in 1790 to visit friends after Rachel's divorce from Leonard Robards. In another version of the tale, Andrew Jackson carried Rachel off to Natchez to get her away from Leonard, who was abusing her. Jackson also hoped that his actions would encourage Leonard to divorce Rachel. At any rate, the couple is said to have arrived at Springfield Plantation in 1791, and Thomas Marston Green Jr. arranged their marriage. The problem with this romantic story is that no record of Rachel and

Andrew Jackson's marriage in Natchez has ever been found. The fact that two of Rachel's nieces were married to members of the Green family could explain why Rachel wanted to be married at Springfield Plantation. Supposedly, Rachel and Andrew spent their weeklong honeymoon in the guest room on the second floor. Because of the lack of hard evidence, the story of Rachel and Andrew Jackson's marriage at Springfield remains a legend. However, this is not the only legend that has been generated inside the old plantation house.

By the 1970s, Springfield seemed destined to fall into ruin, a fate that had befallen so many other antebellum mansions in the Natchez area. The old house was saved by Arthur La Salle, a direct descendant of French explorer René-Robert Cavelier Sieur La Salle. La Salle had read about Springfield when he was sixteen years old. In 1977, he sold his home in Pennsylvania and moved to Natchez, where he made Springfield his permanent home. In the book *Ghosts! Personal Accounts of Modern Mississippi Hauntings* by Sylvia Booth Hubbard, La Salle explained why he never felt lonesome at Springfield. He said that during the restoration of Springfield in 1977, he lived in the kitchen wing with his two sons. One night, a friend of his sons was spending the night at Springfield. The chatter in the kitchen soon became too much for Arthur, so he decided to sleep in the bathroom, which was empty except for a bathtub that had been turned upside down. He had just fallen asleep when he heard heavy footsteps walk across the bedroom floor next to the bathroom. The footsteps stopped right at the bathroom door. Arthur waited a few tense moments for someone to open the door. Finally, the suspense became unbearable. He flung open the door, fully expecting to see an intruder. No one was standing in the doorway.

LaSalle heard other weird noises while living at Springfield. He said that at least once a year on a Sunday afternoon when a large group of people is attending a party at Springfield, the festive atmosphere is shattered by the crash of a large object hitting the floor. LaSalle said that it sounds like someone knocking over a large piece of furniture. Over the years, he has also heard the lilting tones of orchestral music on the west side of the house. He said that it sounds like the kind of music that Rachel and Andrew Jackson would have danced to.

When my wife and I visited Springfield Plantation in August 2009, it was undergoing extensive restoration. Mr. LaSalle had died a few weeks before we arrived, and the house was in the hands of new owners. When he was alive, Arthur E. LaSalle gave tours of his beloved home and regaled visitors with the history and legends of Springfield and the Natchez area. Hopefully, the house that became Arthur's lifework is now his permanent home in the afterlife.

THE BURN

The Burn was built in 1834 by John Walworth. "Burn" is a Scottish word for "brook." A drawing showing the way the home looked in 1834 is on display in the front hall. Walworth's family lived in the Greek Revival home for one hundred years, with the exception for a three-year period during the Civil War when it served as the headquarters of Major Jon P. Coleman. Coleman's name, cut by a diamond, is clearly visible in one of the windowpanes. In the front hall is a photograph of one of the Burn's most illustrious visitors—Ulysses S. Grant—who had his picture taken standing on the porch during the Civil War. The Walworth family returned to their home in 1865 at the end of the war.

In 1978, the Burn was converted into a bed-and-breakfast. The guest rooms are furnished in the fashion of the time to re-create the beauty of the home at the height of its splendor. The house also contains china and a dining

The Burn.

table that belonged to John Walworth's family. The brick walkway leads to a two-acre garden, resplendent with camellias, dogwoods and azaleas. Some guests say that the owners' efforts to re-create the past have succeeded too well.

Guests who have stayed at the bed-and-breakfast claim that the old house is haunted. One of the apparitions is a group of three or four Union soldiers who appear in the back of the swimming pool. The men appear to be deep in conversation. The ghost of a little blond girl is said to disturb the sleep of people in one of the rooms. She could be the ghost of one of the two Walworth children who died in the house during one of the city's outbreaks of yellow fever. Perhaps the process of restoring and converting the old home into a bed-and-breakfast aroused its dormant spirits, a result that seems to be the case in many bed-and-breakfasts throughout the South.

The owners promote the Burn as "history in a cozy setting." Indeed, the rooms come with such twentieth-century amenities as flat-screen televisions, air conditioning and full baths. Guests are treated to wine in the evening and to a full breakfast in the morning consisting of eggs, biscuits, bacon, sausage and fruit. The ghosts are an unadvertised perk.

THE DEVIL'S PUNCHBOWL

The two-hundred-foot-high bluff that runs along the east side of the Mississippi River at Natchez swings inward just north of the Natchez City Cemetery, forming a huge semicircular depression that somewhat resembles an inverted cone. For many years, this deep ravine has been the subject of scores of legends. Some say that Native Americans used this pit as a burial ground. Others say that the Union commander of Natchez enclosed over twenty thousand freed slaves in the Devil's Punchbowl; thousands of them died here. This huge pit has been said to be a favorite hiding place for river pirates and outlaws. A land pirate named John Murrel is rumored to have used the Devil's Punchbowl as headquarters. Two of the Natchez Trace's most infamous outlaws, Big Harpe and Little Harpe, also made this huge hole in the ground their hideout. It is said that after they robbed and murdered their victims, they cut them open, filled their insides with large rocks and heaved their corpses into the Devil's Punchbowl, where they sank beneath the murky water. In modern times, airplanes are said to have crashed inside the Devil's Punchbowl. People say that after thunderstorms, the bones of the people who were buried here float to the surface. Because of all of the deaths that have occurred at the Devil's Punchbowl, many people living in Natchez today believe it is haunted.

The most commonly reported evidence of the presence of ghosts at the Devil's Punchbowl is strange sounds, especially moans. The cries that sometimes echo through the ravine are said to be those of the mistress of an outlaw named Joseph

The Devil's Punchbowl.

Thompson Hare. Legend has it that Hare fell in love with one of the hundreds of the "ladies of the evening" who plied their illicit trade at the saloons and brothels of Natchez-Under-the-Hill. Hare is said to have given her the gold jewels that he stole from travelers on the Natchez Trace in exchange for her fidelity while he was off looking for more victims. One night, after returning to Natchez-Under-the-Hill with a bag full of loot, he heard rumors that his mistress had found comfort in the arms of someone else while he was away. In a fit of rage, he ordered his men to escort the woman to the Devil's Punchbowl and bury her alive with the gold and jewels he had given her. For almost two centuries, people claim to have seen the ghost of a beautiful woman at the Devil's Punchbowl who offered them handfuls of gold and jewels if they relocated her body to a proper burial ground. No record exists of anyone having taken her up on her offer.

Hundreds of people travel to the Devil's Punchbowl, made popular by Greg Iles's novel by the same name. Some come looking for the treasure that John Murrel and the Harpe brothers are said to have buried here. Others come hoping to catch sight of a ghost or two. However, this massive, overgrown depression in the earth is steep and dangerous. The Devil's Punchbowl is private property, owned by David New. A fence has been erected around the borders of the depression to discourage people from risking their lives in search of what is most likely the stuff of legends. The Devil's Punchbowl should be appreciated for what it is: a pristine natural site and a geological anomaly.

THE GARDENS

Sandwiched between Natchez City Cemetery and the National Cemetery is a beautiful example of the planters' cottages of the Lower Mississippi Valley. After receiving a land grant from the Spanish Crown, Stephen Minor decided to take up permanent residence in the region that he had served for so long, first as a captain in the Spanish Royal Armies and then as adjutant major of the post. In 1794, Minor built this imposing twelve-room building with a full-width twelve- by eighty-foot front gallery. People who visited the Gardens for the first time marveled at the wooden wainscoting, the Federal mantels, the large elliptical archway in the hall and the semicircular fanlights over each of the twin front twelve-paneled doorways. The house was certainly befitting the man who would go on to serve as Spanish governor of the Natchez District from 1797 to 1798.

The Gardens.

Several different families have lived in the Gardens over the years. One of the owners, Louise Clarke Purnell, went on to write *Diddle Dumps and Tot*, a children's story about children growing up on a plantation in the antebellum South. In 1881, the Gardens passed into the hands of Louisa Schleet, wife of Charles Daniel Schleet. Descendants of the Schleet family have lived in the Gardens for over a century. The present owner, Dr. Fred Gilbert Emrick, is the great-great-grandson of the Schleets. His wife, Mary Emricks, believes that she and her family have encountered the spirits of her husband's family.

Mary Emrick first became aware of the presence of the ghosts of her in-laws as the result of a very common household event. She was setting out a china bowl owned by her mother-in-law when it slipped out of her hands and fell to the floor, smashing into several pieces. Heartbroken at the loss of her mother-in-law's bowl, Mary set about collecting the china shards that were scattered over the floor. When she examined the pieces that she had collected, Mary was dismayed to discover that a small triangular chip was missing. She looked all over but was unable to find the missing piece. She put the pieces away, convinced that she would never find the missing piece. A few years later, however, the missing piece reappeared.

Mary said:

> *I had just returned home from work when I walked into the dining room and noticed something different about the dining room table. I went over to the table for a closer look, and there, in the middle of the table, was the little triangular chip. I have no idea how it got there.*

Mary also believes that the ghosts of the Schleet family reveal themselves through unexplained noises in the house. "The most common noise is the slamming of doors," Mary said.

> *One Sunday morning, we went home between Sunday school and church. Just as we walked into the house, we heard a door slam in the old part of the house. We ran into the bedroom, thinking that someone had broken into the house in our absence, but no one was there.*

Mary Emrick is not 100 percent convinced that her house is haunted because it has not been certified as being haunted by experts. Most paranormal investigators would agree, though, that the Gardens meets many of the qualifications of a haunted house. An untold number of people have died in the house over the years. Also, the Emricks could have stirred up the spirits when they converted one of the bedrooms in the old part of the house into a bedroom. One should not exclude the possibility, however, that the spirit of Mary's mother-in-law might have returned the missing piece of china as a way of easing her daughter-in-law's guilt over having accidentally damaged a family heirloom.

THE BANK + TRUST COMPANY

Before the old Bank & Trust Company Building was erected on Franklin Street in 1927, several different buildings stood at this site over the course of the city's history. In the 1890s, a hardware store was located here. However, a more insidious building stood here between 1790 and 1815: the Territorial Jail. Hundreds of scoundrels and outlaws were incarcerated here in the jail's twenty-five-year history. Its most infamous detainee was Wiley "Little" Harpe.

In 1797, Little Harpe and his brother, Micajah "Big" Harpe, moved from North Carolina to East Tennessee, where they began stealing livestock from their neighbors in Knox County. The Harpe brothers eventually left Knox County and began robbing and killing people along the

Tennessee and Kentucky border. The brothers made a fatal mistake when they slit the throats of the wife and child of Moses Stegall during a robbery. After Stegall captured and beheaded Big Harpe with a butcher knife in 1799, Little Harpe joined up with an outlaw named Samuel Mason. For five years, Harpe and Mason terrorized travelers along the Natchez Trace. Little Harpe was captured and hanged in 1804 at the Territorial Jail when he tried to collect reward money for turning in the head of Samuel Mason. Many people believe that the ghost of the man who boasted

Exterior of the Bank & Trust Company Building.

of killing forty people is responsible for the paranormal activity at the Bank & Trust Company Building.

For many years, employees of the Bank & Trust Company claimed to have had strange experiences. People complained of feeling someone grab their shoulders or pull their hair when they walked down the stairs to the basement. Just before the bank closed in 1982, the head bank teller was working in the vault when the door suddenly closed and locked on its own. Fortunately, his plight was quickly discovered, and he was released before

The bank vault at the Bank & Trust Company.

running out of air. The door was far too heavy to simply close on its own.

After the bank closed, a restaurant was housed in the building. Pots and pans hanging on the wall in the lobby frequently fell to the floor, seemingly on their own. One day, the employees were getting ready for a reception that was to be held in the lobby. After placing the food on the counter, they went to the back room of the restaurant. When they returned to the lobby, they were shocked to find that all of the plates had slid off the counter and fallen on the floor. The restaurant closed after only one year.

The lobby of the Bank & Trust Company.

For several years, the old Bank & Trust Company building has been a regular stop on the Natchez Ghost Tour. Tourists have photographed an eerie, glowing figure inside the bank. Disembodied voices have been recorded. When I toured the building, my wife, Marilyn, walked around holding a K-2 meter. She said that the meter spiked at several different spots within the building. Little Harpe, it seems, has no intention of leaving the site of his execution.

THE TOWERS

In 1840, Dinah Postlethwaite deeded the acreage on which the Towers now stands to G.O. Blenis. The mansion was redesigned in the Italianate style by J. Edwards Smith for William C. Chamberlain between 1859 and 1860. Chamberlain, who was born and raised in the North, was more interested in creating a southern mansion than in living in one. The Towers became the only antebellum mansion in Natchez with recessed double galleries. In 1861, the Towers was purchased by Mr. and Mrs. Fleming.

Because the Towers was located behind Union lines, it was occupied by the Union army. The officers were quartered inside the mansion, and the soldiers camped out on the lawn. Local legend has it that one of the Union officers quartered here, Peter B. Haynes, was so outraged when one of the Surgets failed to invite him to a dinner party that he ordered the destruction of their mansion. The

The Towers.

mansion, which was also known as Gardenia for the cape jasmine growing along the walks, acquired the name of the Towers because of the two-story rooms at either end of the house. The right tower was removed, and the left tower was destroyed by fire in 1927. The Towers was restored to its nineteenth-century grandeur by a descendant of John Fleming. The mansion's most resilient feature, however, seems to be its signature ghost story.

According to the legend, the Towers is haunted by the ghost of a little girl named Katie. After construction of the house was finished, Katie was playing hide-and-seek with a little friend. Tired of having her hiding places discovered, Katie decided to conceal herself someplace where her friend would never look: a steamer trunk in the attic. Katie had just climbed inside the trunk when the lid slammed shut, locking her in. By the time Katie's family looked inside the trunk, she had suffocated.

For many years, Katie's ghost has forewarned people of impending doom within the house. When Katie's family returned to the Towers after the Civil War, one of her uncles became very sick. As his condition worsened, his family members began hearing rapping noises on the ceiling, walls and doors. They also heard strange scratching sounds from within the walls. When they walked outside, they heard the same noises inside the trees. Three days after the noises began, the uncle died. Four more members of the same family heard the noises until 1910, when they finally moved out of the house.

A number of different people have owned the Towers since 1910. Today, the Towers is a tour home. Visitors are attracted to house from miles around because of its unique furnishings, including gentlemen's mother-of-pearl and ivory watch fobs, Moser glass, 350 antique beaded purses and a collection of props from the 2004 film version of *Phantom of the Opera*. The house is known for its twenty-four bronze sculptures of wildlife, including five bears on the front lawn. One could argue, though, that the Towers' most distinctive touch is the tale of the little girl who accompanies the dying to the other side.

BIBLIOGRAPHY

BOOKS

Brown, Alan. *Haunted Places in the American South*. Jackson: University Press of Mississippi, 2002.

Brown, Dale Campbell, et al. *Stanton Hall: Natchez*. Natchez, MS: Myrtle Bank Publishers, 1980.

Callon, Sim C., and Carolyn Vance Smith. *The Goat Castle Murder*. Natchez, MS: Plantation Publishing Company, 1985.

Estes, Don. *Legends of the Natchez City Cemetery*. Natchez, MS: GraveDigger Publishing, 2009.

Hauck, Dennis William. *Haunted Places: The National Directory*. New York: Penguin Books, 1996.

Hendrix, Margaret Shields. *The Legend of Longwood*. Natchez, MS: Maxwell Printing Corporation, 1972.

Hubbard, Sylvia Booth. *Ghosts! Personal Accounts of Modern Mississippi Hauntings*. Brandon, MS: QRP Books, 1992.

Kempe, Helen Kerr. *The Pelican Guide to Old Homes of Mississippi*. Vol. 1, *Natchez and the South*. Gretna, LA: Pelican Publishing Company, 1989.

Morris, Kathryn E. *Dunleith*. Ridgeland, MS: Hederman Brothers, 2007.

Sinsheimer, Cynthia J. Parker. *Monmouth: Its Majesty and Legacy*. Bogalusa, LA: Delta Printing Company, 2008.

Turnage, Sheila. *Haunted Inns of the Southeast*. Winston-Salem, NC: John F. Blair, 2001.

WEBSITES

Adams County, MS Genealogical and Historical Research. "Natchez City Cemetery: Adams County, MS." www.natchezbelle.org/adams-ind/ncc2.htm.

Briscoe Center for American History. "A Guide to the Surget Family Papers." www.lib.utexas.edu/taro/utcah/0046/cah-0004 6.html.

Edwards, Jennifer. "Local Historian Tells Stories from Natchez City Cemetery in New Book." Natchezdemocrat.com. www.natchezdemocrat.com/news/2009/nov/04local-historian-tells-stories-natchez.

Flickr. "Dunleith Plantation, Natchez, Mississippi." www.flickr.com/photos/jstephenconn/2870462472.

————. "26 Possible Ghost Photograph in the Parlor of Magnolia Hall—Natchez, Mississippi." www.flickr.com/photos/sunnybrook100/556964915.

Geniecorner.com. "Longwood House Natchez, Adams County, Mississippi. www.geniecorner.com/HTML/Longwood.html.

Ghostinmysuitcase.com. "Magnolia Hall: Natchez, MS." www.ghostinmysuitcase.com/places/magnolia/index.htm.

————. "Natchez Under the Hill." www.ghostinmysuitcase.com/places/under/index.htm.

————. "Stories from Natchez City Cemetery." www.ghostinmyusuitcase.com/places/natchez/index.htm.

Grayson, Walt. "Look around Mississippi: Devil's Punch Bowl." www.wlox.com/Global/story.asp?S=11602856.

————. "Natchez City Cemetery." Wlbt.com. www.wlbt.com/Global/story.asp?S=11504256.

HauntedHouses.com. "Monmouth Plantation." www.hauntedhouses.com/states/ms/monmouth.cfm.

Lane, Doris. "America's First Known Serial Killers: The Harpes, Big and Little." www.crimemagazine.com/harps.htm.

Linden Plantation Gardens. "A History of Linden Plantation and Gardens." www.lindenplantationgardens.com/history.htm.

Mississippibeautiful.com. "Longwood Plantation—Natchez, Mississippi." www.mississippibeautiful.com/capital-river/longwood-plantation.html.

Natchezcitycemetery.com. "Welcome to the Natchez City Cemetery." www.natchezcitycemetery.com/custom/webpage.cfm?content=content&id=2.

Natchez on the River. "Don't Believe in Ghosts? Think Again." www.natchezontheriver.com/news/2008/oct/27/dont-believe-ghosts-think-again.

———. "Stanton Hall." www.natchezontheriver.com/news/1008/oct/13/stanton-hall.

———. "Stanton Hall: Natchez's Premier Attraction Is a Destination Wedding Dream Come True." www.stantonhall.com/index.html.

Natchez Things To Do. "Old Adams County Jail." www.virtualtourist.com/travel/North_America/United_States_of_america/Mississipi.

Natchez-Under-the-Hill Saloon. "A Little of Under-the-Hill." www.underthehillsaloon.com/custom/webpage.cfm?content=News&id=46.

National Historic Landmarks Program. "Arlington." http://tps.cr.nps.gov/nhl/detail.cfm?ResourceId=1342&ResourceType=Building.

Taylor, Troy. "Dead Men Do Tell Tales." Goat Castle. www.prairieghosts.com/goat.html.

———. "Haunted Mississippi: Ghosts of Natchez, Natchez, Mississippi." www.prairieghosts.com/natchez/html.

———. "To the Devil, I Say!" www.prairieghosts.com/devilnames.html.

Towersofnatchez.com. "History of the Towers." http://thetowersofnatchez.com/history.html.

Travelblog.org. "Springfield Plantation." www.travelblog.org/North-America/United States/Mississippi/Springfield-Plantation.

Tylersterritory.com. "Stanton Hall, Natchez, Mississippi." www.tylersterritory.com/travel/namerica/mississippi/antebellum/stantonhall-01.html.

Wikipedia. "Arlington (Natchez, Mississippi)." http://en.wikipedia.org/wiki/Arlington-(Natchez,_Mississippi).

———. "John Murrell (bandit)." http://wikipedia.org/wiki/John_Murrell_(bandit).

———. "Longwood (Natchez, Mississippi." http://en.wikipedia.org/wiki/Longwood_(Natchez,_Mississippi).

NEWSPAPERS

Rucker, LaReeca. "Ghosts in the House: Tales of the Supernatural Get Top Billing on Halloween." *Clarion Ledger*, October 31, 2008, sec. 3D.